Homecoming Magic at Christmas

Also by Suzanne Stengl

~ ghosts and angels ~

The Ghost and Christie McFee

Angel Wings

The Thurston Heirloom

~ sweet contemporary romance series ~

A Wedding and a White Christmas

On the Way to a Wedding

Wedding Bell Blues

Homecoming Magic at Christmas

A SWEET ROMANCE NOVELLA

SUZANNE STENGL

Publisher: Mya & Angus
Cover Design: GetCovers

www.suzannestengl.com

MYA & ANGUS

To Bob ☺

Homecoming Magic *at* Christmas

Every year on the second Saturday of December, the Bonninghams hosted their annual Christmas party, and this year would be no different. Except, maybe, for the number of guests that would attend.

The Bonninghams, Claire and Brent, owned the large, modern house at the end of Maple Street in the small town of Gravelton. They also owned the grocery store, the hardware store and the funeral parlor.

This year, their son and their daughter had both come home to Gravelton for the holidays, and so had a number of their old friends from high school.

Julie Sutherland was one of them.

Six and a half years ago, she had left the little town—immediately following their high school graduation party which, like every other big event in the town, had been held at the Bonninghams' landmark home.

That night, Julie had worn the silver dress that fit her so well—and that had cost so much. She had spent an hour putting on makeup and fixing her hair. For days, she'd practiced walking in the strappy silver sandals that complemented her shimmering outfit.

She'd arrived early at the Bonninghams' house, anxious to see her boyfriend, because they'd decided to meet there, at the party. Her world had been perfect as she'd stood inside the wide foyer waiting for him to appear.

It was as if the universe had managed to nudge all the pieces into place—and to create a magical end to her high school years. She could not have wished for more.

But, as the minutes…and then an hour…and then another ticked by, it became apparent, even to her. That night, with all of her classmates to witness it, the boy of her dreams had stood her up.

. . . . .

Julie came down the stairs at her parents' home, wearing her red sweater and black pants, and carrying a pair of black ballet flats. Her boots stood by the door. She'd need them since it was snowing, and the forecast was calling for more snow. Good thing she'd arrived yesterday, before this storm started.

Her mother met her in the small entrance. "Have you got a date tonight?"

Julie dropped her flats into a red canvas bag with a poinsettia motif. "No," she said. "I'm going with Rob and a friend of his."

"Oh!" Her mother's eyes widened. "I didn't know he was home for the holidays. I thought the hospital would need him."

"He got time off this year." In fact, they'd sat together on the bus for the long ride home.

"Little Robbie," her mother mused. "It's been so long since I've seen that boy."

"He's hardly *little Robbie* anymore." Not at six foot two.

"Always a handful, that one."

He probably had been, Julie thought. All she could remember was that her next-door neighbor had been a major source of irritation while she was growing up. But, he'd gradually become more tolerable as they'd made their way through elementary school, and then through high school.

"I still remember that time he talked you into climbing up the ladder onto the garage. And, poor little thing, you couldn't get down." Her mother smiled, and then, perhaps worried about more mishaps, she added, "Don't let him get you into any trouble tonight!"

"Don't worry, Mom. He's a grown-up now."

After graduation, a handful of their friends had stayed in Gravelton. The rest of the class had left town—some to volunteer, some to travel, some to serve in the military, but most to go to college. Julie and Rob had both gone to Rosamond College in New Breckenhill, and since New Breckenhill and the college were both small, they often ran into each other.

But she hadn't seen many of her other high school friends in a long time. Actually—she winced—not since the night of the infamous graduation party.

"Are you walking over?"

"No, Rob's parents are driving. We're all going together."

"I doubt his parents will stay long."

"They won't," Julie said, as she slipped on her coat. "They're worried it'll be too noisy."

"Yes, I think it will. You'll walk home?"

"Sure. Walking in the snow will be fun."

"Mmm, hmm." Her mother nodded.

Julie could feel some advice coming on.

"I wish you'd got a date for tonight." Her mother wrung her hands. "I still remember your grad night, dear. You were so disappointed."

"I don't have anything to prove, Mom." And it would be so lovely if her mother would please let that horrible night rest.

"But don't you think it would be better if you showed up with a date this time?"

Julie opened her mouth to respond, but what was there to say? Fortunately, right at that moment, the doorbell chimed.

Saved by the bell.

"Oh well," her mother conceded. "At least, you're *going* to the party this year."

Julie came home every Christmas, but she'd never gone back to the annual Christmas party.

Until now.

She opened the door.

· · · · ·

Rob stood on the porch, with snowflakes dusting his dark brown hair. He wore the gray parka and the black snow boots he'd been wearing on the bus. Julie noticed he'd changed out of jeans, in favor of navy pants.

Since he usually wore scrubs all day, the navy pants would be his attempt to look more *dressed up* for the party.

He also sported a red and white striped scarf, wound several times around his neck. A candy cane scarf. That would be his attempt at *festive* for Christmas.

Although, knowing Rob, he might be wearing one of those ridiculous Christmas sweaters under his parka.

"Come in. Come in." Her mother motioned with a hand.

Rob stepped inside, stomping snow on the mat. "Hello, Mrs. Sutherland."

"Hello, Robbie." Julie's mother strained her

neck to look up at him. "My goodness! You're getting so tall!"

Seriously? Julie grimaced. Rob must be sick of hearing that comment from the old towners. She sent a quick glance his way.

He shrugged and laughed, probably used to it.

"Everything going well at school?"

"Second year of residency. I'll be a full-fledged doctor soon."

Julie's mother smiled a look of confusion. Rob had not seemed academically inclined growing up. Somehow he'd managed to hide that part of himself.

"How are your parents? I hear they're going to the party."

"For an hour or so. They want to put in an appearance. Are you going?"

"We thought about it." She bowed her head. "But Herbert is still getting over a cold so we're going to skip this year."

Julie stepped into her boots.

"And, with all you young people home, I'm sure the house will be full to the brim."

"Then I hope to see you later in the holidays."

Somewhere along the line, Rob had learned to be polite. Julie wasn't quite sure when that had happened but it had. With her poinsettia bag dangling from her arm, she zipped up her coat. "Let's go," she said.

The sooner the better. At any moment, her mother would dig up a childhood story and start retelling it.

"Have a good time," her mother said. "Say hello to Claire and Brent, and tell them we're sorry we couldn't make it."

"Sure thing, Mom."

. . . . .

Outside, Julie let go of a breath. At least, her mother had not mentioned *that night* to Rob. Although, he most likely remembered it.

And, good thing, too, that her parents were *not* coming tonight. They wouldn't be staring at her for her first appearance back at—she briefly closed her eyes—at the scene of the crime.

Next door, Rob's father—Mr. McKinley—was sweeping snow off his old Buick. The car was running, warming up. They'd leave soon, but Rob still stood at her porch.

She looked up at him.

"You're nervous."

"I'm not." So he *did* remember. Of course, he would. "Really. I'm not. Rory won't be there."

For some reason, that seemed hard to believe. Rob raised a brow. "And you know this because?"

"Linda told me." Linda, who knew all the town gossip. "Rory won't be there."

"Okay." A slow nod. Then Rob zeroed in on her eyes. "If he is, do you want me to take out his knees?"

"Don't be silly. I'm fine."

He put an arm around her shoulders and gave her a squeeze. "Come on."

Five minutes later, she was tucked between Rob and his friend Matthew in the backseat of the Buick. Matthew worked for the Bonninghams at the hardware store. He gripped a huge box of chocolates in his mittened hands. A bright red bow decorated the top.

"Never thought you'd come back to one of these parties," Matthew said.

Julie glared at him. She hadn't been a close friend of Matthew's—he was Rob's friend—but since Matthew remembered...*the night in question*...that meant probably everyone at the party would also remember.

Just wonderful. It was going to take some major Christmas magic to get through tonight.

"Everybody buckled in?" Rob's father called from the driver's seat.

In the tight quarters and with their bulky coats, Julie struggled to find the seatbelt latch. Her shoe bag threatened to slip off her lap.

"Hold this," Rob said, handing her the large bottle of Baileys Irish Cream. It had been lying on the seat when he'd opened the door.

A second later, he pulled the seatbelt around her, and snapped it into the clip. She returned the Baileys to him.

The heater roared and the wipers beat a rhythm,

clearing the windshield. Still snowing.

"Are you sure you'll be all right?" Mr. McKinley asked. "Walking home in this?"

"Don't worry, Dad. It's supposed to clear after midnight."

Mr. McKinley's head bobbed once. Twice. "Of course," he said. "After midnight." His jaw tightened. "You young people." Another quick nod, and then, "Where's your mother?"

At last, Rob's mother, Mrs. McKinley, opened the front passenger door.

"Oh! There you are, Julie! Welcome home! Can you hold this for me?" She passed a large tray wrapped in clear plastic.

"Hello, Mrs. McKinley." Julie dropped her shoe bag on the floor and took the tray, balancing it on her lap. Gingerbread cookies. Gingerbread boys and girls. Gingerbread stars and trees.

Belatedly, she realized she'd forgotten. With all the running around today, with visiting her aunt and her cousins, with helping her mother get groceries, with decorating the tree, and, finally, with a quick visit to the hardware store to check in with Linda—who worked there—and to confirm that Rory would *not* be at the party tonight, with all of that, Julie had completely forgotten about bringing the obligatory social offering.

She sighed. Points against her already.

Rob's mother did up her seatbelt, and Rob's father started inching the Buick out of the driveway.

Mrs. McKinley angled her head toward the back. "Julie! My goodness! It's been so long since we've seen you!"

"I know," Julie apologized. Why did she feel like she needed to apologize? "I've been getting home, but just for short visits. School is busy."

"You're still at that same college? Rosamond? The one Rob used to go to?"

Rob still spent time at Rosamond, but mostly he was at Mercy Hospital. No use explaining that. "Yes, that's where I am. I'm a research assistant now, while I work on my Master's."

"Oh, my. So *much* education. And what will you finally do? For work, I mean?"

"I…" It was hard to explain the intricacies of her work to a lay person. "I will study hearts," she said.

That satisfied Mrs. McKinley.

But not Rob. He leaned close to her. "*Study hearts?* Really?"

"Then you explain it."

· · · · ·

Soon, they were at the Bonninghams' house, and Julie slumped. Maybe her mother had been right? Maybe it would have been a good idea to show up with a date?

But…there was no one to *be* her date. No one she could have brought home from New

Breckenhill, and certainly no one in this town.

Sure, she had met boyfriends at Rosamond College, but none of those relationships had taken.

Mr. McKinley found a parking spot along the street.

Rob, holding the bottle of Baileys, got out of the car and waited by the door for Julie to shuffle across. She had her shoe bag looped over her arm as she balanced the tray of cookies. It would be a disaster to drop them.

By the time she was out of the car, Matthew had come around to their side, carefully holding on to his gift of chocolates.

"I'm kinda hoping Penelope Jane didn't come home," he said, a tone of dejection in his voice.

Rob grinned at him. "I'm afraid she did."

Julie still carried the tray of gingerbread cookies. Should she pass it back to Mrs. McKinley? After all, it wouldn't be fair to take credit for the baking.

But no, not yet. Because Mrs. McKinley took her husband's arm as they started walking along the driveway toward the house, moving cautiously on the packed snow.

Happy for the grip her boots provided, Julie walked between Rob and Matthew, and still wished she had thought to bring something. *Anything.*

Tall, imposing evergreens lined the long driveway and snow weighed on the branches.

Closer now, she saw the heavy brick columns that framed the wide entrance, and a large wooden snowman that stood next to…a new door.

It was not surprising.

Claire and Brent Bonningham always scouted for ways to make their home look more impressive.

They had chosen an arched door made of dark wood. Probably going for Old World charm. The door had a large inset panel on the bottom and glass panes above. Strips of wrought iron divided the glass into tall sections. As the iron reached the upper part of the glass, it twisted into curly details.

Covering much of the door's window was a huge Christmas wreath.

They'd reached the three steps that led up to the porch. That is, she and Rob and Matthew had reached the steps. Rob's parents were slowly advancing along the driveway.

"Let's wait on the porch," Rob said, and up they went.

Now they could hear the music, or rather, the bass beat of an unrecognizable song as it thumped out a rhythm. Julie almost expected to see the solid wood door vibrate and pulse, like one of those large speakers people had for their stereo systems.

She glanced back at Rob's parents. Mrs. McKinley seemed to be having trouble with her balance on the slippery parts of the driveway. It would have been a good idea to drop her at the door.

At least, Julie thought, this delayed the moment when she would have to enter, bringing only her shoes to the party.

She turned and studied the wreath. It was made of real cedar and pine, the scent filling the cold night air. Red balls and gold balls and sprigs of holly berries decorated the evergreen. Instead of a bow, a large poinsettia anchored the bottom.

The holly berries looked real. The poinsettia was artificial.

The wreath must have been ordered online and delivered to the house, since it was unlikely that something this grand could be found at Gretta's Variety Store.

In contrast, the wooden snowman was friendly and welcoming. He was made of white painted boards—white except for the rosy cheeks, and the black top hat, and the black mittens clasped over a large belly. And for a bit more color, there was a red and gold striped scarf around his neck.

He held an old-fashioned broom with straw bristles in the shape of a fan. His nose was long and carrot-orange. His eyes were coal-colored, perhaps made of real pieces of coal. In the light from the porch, the eyes glittered. And winked, with a touch of Christmas magic.

Finally, Rob's parents reached the porch. Matthew rang the bell. Julie handed the tray of cookies to Mrs. McKinley.

. . . . .

A moment later, the door was jerked open by Penelope Jane Bonningham. She was pretty, two years junior to Rob and Julie, and annoying. At least, she had been annoying when Julie had last seen her.

And the last time Julie had seen her was here, at that graduation party…when Julie had just finished grade twelve and Penelope Jane had just finished grade ten. Hopefully the girl had matured since then.

"Ugh!" Penelope Jane said, her voice loud over the pounding music. "I thought it would be *my* friends."

So then, not matured.

"Woodley's in the rumpus room," Penelope Jane said, flicking her bottle blond hair over her shoulder.

In the same class as Rob and Julie, Woodley had been only slightly more gracious than his sister.

Penelope Jane turned, took two steps away from them, and stopped. She spun around. "Hey! Aren't you…" She circled a finger, searching her memory. "You're the one who went crazy that time." She stabbed her finger in Julie's direction. "When your boyfriend didn't show. Rory! I remember now. Wow! You came back! I can't believe it!"

Julie felt Rob's arm tighten around her shoulders.

"Woodley will love this." Penelope Jane smiled broadly. "Go find him," she said, and she disappeared, leaving them unattended.

"What a peculiar girl," Mrs. McKinley noted.

They stepped out of the cold, through the

doorway and into the stately foyer which featured a dark green tiled floor with a custom gold-colored inlay. Penelope Jane had raved about it when it was first installed. Julie focused on the pattern of the tile, willing her cheeks not to heat up.

A few seconds later, an old woman leaning on a silver cane wobbled toward the entrance. She wore a long black satin dress trimmed with white lace around the collar.

The grandmother?

"Hello!" the old lady greeted them, speaking above the noise. "Welcome! And Merry Christmas!" She spotted Mrs. McKinley's baking. "Oh my stars! Those look delicious!"

"Fresh from the oven." Mrs. McKinley beamed.

"Hello, Mrs. Bonningham," Matthew said. "I'm—"

"I remember you, Matthew." Old lady Bonningham sent him a kind smile. "You were here last year, weren't you?"

"Yes, I was," Matthew answered. Since Matthew lived in Gravelton, he attended yearly. "And this is—"

"Ahh! You brought chocolates! You dear boy." Then she eyed Rob and Julie. "And you are?"

"This is Julie. And this is Rob," Matthew said. "They were also in Woodley's class."

"That's wonderful," old lady Bonningham said. "Maybe you can talk to him about playing something more…" She paused a moment and her eyebrows lifted. "Christmas-y?"

. . . . .

Rob took coats from his parents and boots were removed.

Old lady Bonningham—Woodley and Penelope Jane's grandmother—assigned coat duty to Matthew since...*you remember where the study is, don't you, dear?*

And, even though Matthew seemed to insist on calling her Mrs. Bonningham, she told them all to call her Spade, since *everyone else does*.

She led Rob's parents to the kitchen, with his mother carrying the cookies, and his father carrying the chocolates and the Baileys.

"The study's this way," Matthew said.

"I remember," Julie told him. Even though it had been six years, the study was hard to forget. She grimaced. The whole house was hard to forget.

Matthew dropped his coat on the floor, just inside the door of the study. "I'll see you downstairs," he said. "Woodley has a new pool table." And then Matthew was gone.

As in other years, coats were piled everywhere— on the heavy mahogany desk, in heaps along the walls, and in the closet. The early guests got dibs on the closet.

Rob didn't care.

He slipped three bulky coats off their hangers, letting them drop to the closet floor. Then he hung up the coats he'd taken from his parents.

As he was taking off his own coat, Julie noticed that he was *not* wearing a Christmas sweater, ugly or otherwise. Instead he wore a polo shirt, navy, a shade darker than his pants.

It still seemed strange to see him out of scrubs. In New Breckenhill, they often met for coffee, usually at one of the cafeterias at Rosamond College or at Mercy Hospital. And, of course, he always wore scrubs there.

"Give me your coat."

She did.

He dropped one more coat to the closet floor and used the hanger.

The pile on the floor resembled a cozy nest, and Julie wished she could curl up on it. And hide.

"You *are* nervous," Rob said.

"I shouldn't have come."

"Of course, you should have come. That's ancient history."

"Not to Penelope Jane."

"She's special," Rob said. And then he did something he'd never done before. At least, not since they were about six years old.

He took her hand. "Let's get ourselves some Christmas cheer." He tugged her out of the study and back into the foyer.

Julie noticed the ornate French doors on her left,

and beyond them, the formal dining room, empty and quiet. She stopped to look inside, not ready to go any farther. Rob waited next to her.

A tall Christmas tree—maybe six feet tall—stood at the end of the dining room. Blue and white decorations hung from the branches: blue balls, white doves, blue and white twisted ribbons. And, on top, a large blue star.

It looked perfect, like something from the pages of a magazine.

"Come on," Rob said, quietly. "Christmas cheer? Remember? We're almost there."

He nudged her away from the French doors, until they stood on the threshold of the great room. Their old classmates grouped in clusters with drinks in hand, talking and gesturing. No one had noticed her. Not yet.

Two steps led down from the foyer. Rob still held her hand. They were ready to descend into the chaos of the party.

Straight ahead, in front of the dark floor-to-ceiling windows, stood *another* Christmas tree. This one, even taller. And this one had a red and green theme with a large *red* star on top.

It was as if the Bonninghams couldn't agree on how to decorate this year's tree. So to avoid the argument, they'd put up two trees.

But would Santa know where to leave the presents?

On the right side of the great room, bookshelves

lined the wall. And, at the end of that wall, a corner fireplace flickered weakly, in need of attending.

To their left, the great room opened to the kitchen and dining nook. Between the great room and the kitchen, the handrail and balusters of the staircase poked up from the rumpus room below. That was where the loud blaring was coming from.

They were still standing between the foyer and the great room, at the top of the steps. On the brink of the party. She felt Rob squeeze her hand.

"Look," he said, glancing up.

She did, and—

Wasn't that pretty? A sprig of mistletoe dangled above their heads.

"Want me to kiss you?"

"What?" Julie stepped back as a fluttery feeling tingled through her belly.

"People can think we're together," Rob said. "Like boyfriend, girlfriend." He looked her straight in the eye. "It will ease your homecoming."

It might. But, naturally, Rob was only joking.

"I don't care what people think."

Except, she did care. Very much.

· · · · ·

And then Rob was pulling her along and somehow she made it across the great room without bumping into anyone.

But why did they call it a great room? It did not feel like a great room because she certainly did not *feel* great.

She felt watched. Like every eye at the party was watching her. Like every topic of conversation had suddenly become about her. And about that embarrassing night of so long ago.

"Punch?"

"What did you say?"

"Here. Take a sip."

Rob fit a little cup into her hands.

She noticed, with embarrassment, that her hands shook. Thankfully, he didn't comment.

They were in the dining nook beside the punch bowl which sat on the nook's wooden table. The kind of wood that was distressed to make it look informal, and therefore, welcoming and cozy—in an otherwise overwhelming setting.

The clear glass punch bowl held a mixture of orange slices, lime slices and cranberries in a bright red liquid.

A piece of holly floated on top of the brew. Julie touched it, to see if it was real holly.

It was. *Real.*

"You're not supposed to eat that," Rob said. "That's for decoration."

She knew that. Of course.

Little glasses surrounded the bowl, some already filled. Between the glasses, someone had strewn— in a seemingly random pattern—some little candy canes, a few red wooden stars and some tiny green bells.

Next to the punch bowl, a centerpiece of pine and pinecones dominated the table. Strings of red beads wove through the pine.

All of it breathed perfection, like a spread for a magazine. Julie looked around, expecting a photographer to be there covering the event.

Rob touched her hands, which still cradled the little cup. "Take a drink," he said.

She did. A tiny sip.

It landed in her stomach with a jolt. "Whoa." She coughed. "That's strong!"

Rob picked up a nearby bottle. It was a short bottle, round on one side, flat on the other, and with a tall neck.

Julie leaned next to him as they read the label together. A gold label that said *Bonne Nuit* in large white letters. Below that, in a smaller font, *Brandy*. And below that, in a still smaller font, *Product of France*.

"Oh dear," said a voice behind them. "I hope my granddaughter didn't put too much alcohol in that."

Old Mrs. Bonningham—that is, *Spade*—had appeared next to the punch bowl.

In her long black dress, she looked anachronistic, like something out of a Victorian novel. Definitely not like someone who fit in here with all the other revelers.

Rob upended the brandy bottle over the punch

bowl. A couple of drops fell in, with a plink.

"Too late," he said. "I think she did."

"Yes," Julie said. "I think Penelope Jane likes it strong."

"Oh my stars!" Spade laughed. "Call her Penny."

No one in their right mind called Penelope Jane *Penny*. At least, none of her contemporaries ever had.

"I know," Spade said, as if she were reading Julie's mind. "Unfortunately, Penny has grown up to be…" A short pause. "Well, I'll just say it. She's grown up to be an entitled little brat."

Julie laughed and took another sip of the potent punch. This time it tasted…smoother.

"Do you see her often?" Rob asked.

"For holidays," Spade said. "Now that I live in Gravelton, I see her whenever she comes home for holidays."

"When did you move to Gravelton?" Rob asked.

"Last year." A crisp nod. "Claire and Brent asked me if I wanted to live with them. And it's worked out well," she said, with a slow smile. "Lord knows the house is big enough for all sorts of people to live here."

"Oh, look!" Julie spied another bottle. Tall and white, this one was stashed behind the pinecone centerpiece.

"Summer Island Estate Rare Blend," she read aloud. Under that was a big numeral *12*. "12 year old," she said. Somehow that was fascinating. She wasn't sure why.

"Rum?" Spade asked.

"Yes, rum." Or *ron*. Or *rhum*. Depending on your language preference.

Spade frowned. "Empty?"

Julie shook the bottle over the punch bowl. Nothing fell out. Not a single drop. "Yes."

Oh well. So the punch had lots of rum and brandy in it. Might as well finish off her little cup. She tipped back the rest of the drink with a hard swallow, then licked her lips.

Now that she was getting used to it, the punch didn't seem that strong.

"Maybe Penelope Jane didn't realize how much alcohol she was adding," Rob said.

"Penny." Spade sent him a stern look.

"Yes, Penny," he agreed, smiling at her.

Spade let her shoulders fall slightly. She stroked her throat, as if she were lost in thought. "Maybe," she said, looking into the distance, "maybe some Christmas magic will touch that little girl."

Rob shook his head. "It might take more than that."

"Don't dismiss Christmas magic, Rob. It can be quite powerful."

· · · · ·

Julie half listened to the exchange between Rob and

Spade. Because, now that she'd finished her drink, she felt a little woozy.

It was probably time to find something to eat, to balance the alcohol. She'd check out the trays of food in the kitchen.

But first, she turned toward the great room and studied the red and green Christmas tree in front of the dark windows. In the daylight, those windows looked out over endless fields—the reason for building the Bonninghams' house on the edge of town—the spectacular view. Although, right now, that view was black.

Rob and Spade were talking again, but Julie was no longer listening.

The noise, or rather the music, still pounded over the whole house. But it seemed like the noise had become more bearable, when combined with the alcohol that eased into her brain.

Above the music, Julie sorted out another sound. A voice. One she knew.

It was her old high school friend Linda. And then Julie saw her. She was coming up the stairs. Unassuming Linda—in a slinky red dress.

What?

Not possible. That couldn't be her old friend. Linda never dressed like that. Not practical, sensible Linda.

As she came up the stairs she was laughing, and talking to someone who was following her up.

A head of tousled blond hair appeared behind

the balusters. Someone in a dark black suit. A dashing black suit. Someone who looked like every girl's dream of the gallant hero.

Rory.

Julie felt a solid coldness expand inside her whole body.

"He's here." She grabbed Rob's arm. "I'm leaving." She slammed her punch glass on the table and without another thought, she found herself weaving across the great room between the clusters of party people.

Past the red and green Christmas tree, up the steps to the foyer, past the French doors of the empty dining room, and finally to the study where her coat was stashed in the closet.

"Julie. Wait."

Rob had followed her.

And from the hall, from far away, another voice. Linda's voice. "Julie! I can explain!"

Julie yanked open the closet door, thought about finding her coat, and gave up. She squeezed inside the closet, pulling the door closed behind her.

The door opened again. Rob. He quickly closed the door and together they scrunched against the coats hanging in there. They heard Linda's voice, muffled by the door. "Julie?" Nothing for a few seconds. "Where did she go?"

In the dark, Julie felt Rob's body beside hers.

A reassuring presence. And that, combined with the effects of the rum and brandy, made her want to laugh. She put her hand over her mouth, trying to be quiet. She could feel him doing the same thing, trying to stifle a laugh. They bumped into each other. He tried to steady her, but she lost her balance, and they tumbled to the floor of the closet, landing on the heap of coats he'd dropped there earlier.

And then, a whack of Christmas magic hit them, and they fell through the floor.

. . . . .

There was a moment of disorientation. Brilliant flashes of light, and then darkness. More flashes of light. Red and green lights, followed by blue and white lights.

Suddenly Julie was back in the dining nook, standing next to the punch bowl. And Rob was gone.

But Spade was there, standing regally in her black satin dress.

"What happened?" Julie asked, turning around, looking for Rob. And then she noticed she was still holding the empty punch glass. She stared at it. "What is *in* this stuff?"

"It's only rum and brandy, dear," Spade said. "But don't argue with Christmas magic."

Magic? Is this what magic felt like? Or is this what being very drunk felt like?

She looked across the room, toward the stairs. No sign of Rory.

And, no sign of Linda.

Linda, who knew *all* the town gossip.

Every year when Julie came home for Christmas, she checked with Linda. Checked to see if Rory would be attending the annual Bonningham Christmas party.

And every year, according to Linda, he was. Except for this year. This was the first time Linda had said Rory would not be here. How could Linda have got it wrong?

Maybe she hadn't got it wrong… Maybe Julie had imagined seeing him?

Had she imagined seeing Linda, too?

An older gentleman approached the punch bowl. He had a round chubby face and thick black hair, not a gray hair in sight.

Julie had the most peculiar sensation that she'd seen him before. And not too long ago.

He was dressed…oddly. All in white. Well, mostly. A white jacket and pants, and a white shirt. To break up the whiteness, he wore a red and gold striped tie.

His shoes were black and—that was strange— he wore black mittens. Not black gloves, which would have been odd enough, even at this party, but black mittens.

Maybe his hands were cold?

His cheeks were rosy and his nose was orangey

red, like he'd been outside in the cold.

Or like he *had* a cold.

But his eyes were welcoming and friendly. And very dark. In the low light of the dining nook, his eyes seemed to glitter like dark pieces of coal.

"Hello, Spade," he said.

"Hello, Charlie," Spade greeted him.

"Julie, this is Charlie," Spade said. "Charlie Frost."

Julie shook hands with the old man, clasping his mittened hand. He felt cold, even through the mitten.

"I need this punch," Charlie said, as he ladled a glass for himself. He drank some, and considered it. "Hmm… Needs to be a little stronger," he said.

And then he considered *her*.

"So, you are Julie."

"Yes, I am." She lifted her chin. Had he heard about her, too?

"Do you think they still care about that?" he asked. And then he answered himself. "They don't," he said. "Well, except for Penny, but her time will come."

Julie didn't particularly like Penny, that is, Penelope Jane. But she didn't wish her any harm.

"At any rate," Charlie continued, "that night when you got stood up? That's old news. No one cares."

Of course, they do. But Julie didn't interrupt Charlie. And he didn't seem to care that he was having a one-sided conversation.

"Though they *have* heard you are doing well in New Breckenhill. You'll be one of those PhD doctors soon enough."

In a couple more years, she thought. Though it seemed like ages before that would happen. Good thing the getting there was enjoyable. She liked her work.

And, she thought, she really should add to this conversation. "You don't think they remember a screaming teenager?"

"Not screaming," he said, with a kind tone in his voice. "You were weeping." The old man heaved a sigh and a thoughtful expression crossed his chubby face. "Although," he went on, "you probably felt like screaming."

"I made a spectacle of myself."

"Most of them understood." He sipped some of his punch. "They never liked Rory in the first place and they wondered what you saw in him." He brushed his mittened hand over his chin. "It was a good thing he didn't come that night. He didn't deserve you."

"Ah! But she still thinks about what might have been." Another person had joined them at the punch bowl. "Don't you, sweetheart?"

The newcomer was a distinctive and striking woman—older than Julie, younger than Spade. Somewhere in her late thirties or early forties.

"Hello, Spade."

"Hello, Aretha."

Aretha was tall, with a commanding presence. The kind of woman who would be cool, confident and collected. No matter the situation.

She would never break down and weep.

Aretha had glowing black skin, perfectly arched brows, and dark, braided hair.

She wore a cherry red, long-sleeved blouse, the same color pants and a beautiful shawl—a silky green shawl with a Christmas pattern of cedar and pine and holly berries.

Tiny red and gold balls dangled from her ears. Her long nails were the color of holly berries. At her throat was a large pin, a poinsettia pin.

"Julie, this is Aretha. Aretha Jaye."

"Nice to meet you," Julie said.

"Nice to finally meet you," Aretha said, with a nod of her head. "And you can forget about that useless piece of—"

Spade coughed.

"I know, Spade. She has to make up her own mind. But, good heavens, some men are not worth pining over."

"I am," Charlie said, moving closer to Aretha.

"Of course you are, Charlie." She sent him a bright smile. "You have lasted the test of time. We always did go well together." She winked at him.

His rosy cheeks grew more rosy.

Was he blushing?

"Have you seen punch?" Aretha asked.

"It's right in front of you," Julie said, wondering what it was about Aretha that seemed so strange…and yet so familiar.

"No, not *the* punch. *Punch*. He's a friend of ours," Aretha said. "You'll like him."

Julie had that peculiar sensation again. The feeling that she'd met Aretha before. And recently.

The noise of the party had subsided. It was still there, but it was as if someone had turned down a radio station. It had been so loud before, but now Julie could only hear the noise in the background.

Which made her wonder if this could all be a dream…

But, on second thought, no. Not a dream, because she felt fully awake.

Then again, although *Spade* seemed real enough, Aretha and Charlie did not. There was something about those two. Something about Aretha and Charlie that was…off.

Julie snuck a glance at them as they leaned close together, staring at the punch bowl.

Oh well, it was probably nothing. Just the brandy and rum muddling her thinking.

All at once, she felt a little tingling at the base of her neck.

Someone else had joined them at the punch bowl. Another odd character. Another older man. But where Charlie had dark hair, this man had red hair. A full head of wavy red hair.

This man wore a royal blue jersey with a white

maple leaf on the front of it. His baggy pants were the same color blue. He also wore a clear plastic belt over the jersey so that the blue of his jersey showed behind the clear belt.

A strange belt—and not just because it was clear, but because it had several hooks hanging from it. Each of the hooks held something: a pair of dice, a tiny hockey stick, a silver pocket knife, a small ornate glass cup, a sprig of holly.

"Julie," Spade said. "This is Georgie."

"Call me Punch," Georgie said.

Georgie, aka Punch, took Julie's empty cup and refilled it.

She didn't want another drink, but she held on to the little cup. *Who has a name like Punch?*

"I'll show you something," Punch said.

"Show me what?"

"What you need to know."

What I need to know? Julie swallowed and her mind raced as she tried to figure out what was going on.

"Come over here."

Julie moved closer to the punch bowl.

"Look here."

"Where?"

"In the punch bowl," he said.

. . . . .

Green and red lights flashed, followed by blue and

white lights, and Julie had that feeling of disorientation again—the same feeling as a few minutes ago, when she'd fallen through the floor of the closet, with Rob.

Where *was* he?

"Look in the punch bowl," the strange man said.

She did. She stared at the punch bowl, at the surface of the bright red liquid.

"See the rumpus room?" Punch asked.

"Is that the rumpus room?"

"Yes, it is," he said.

"How come we can see it?"

"Would you like to see something else?"

"Ahhh, not really," she answered, wishing Rob was here. Rob always made sense of things.

"Look!" Punch gestured at the surface of the punch bowl again. "There's Rob and his friend Matthew."

Julie could see them, standing near the pool table. How, she didn't know, but she could. Then the surface of the punch bowl rippled and the image was gone.

"Oh! Look at that!" Punch said with a wide grin. "There's Rory! Your old boyfriend!"

Julie could see through the surface of the punch bowl again, and, sure enough, there was Rory, wearing that dashing black suit. He stood next to the pool table, leaning against it, arms folded, looking so in charge.

"He got a promotion this year," Punch said.

"A promotion?"

"They made him one of the evening managers at the hardware store."

"The *hardware* store?" Julie set her drink on the table and rubbed her forehead, trying to understand.

"You know, that store on Main Street?"

"I know where the hardware store is. I just didn't know he worked there."

"Where did you think he worked?"

"I never thought about it. But he couldn't be working at the hardware store."

"Why not?"

"Because Linda works at the hardware store."

Punch shrugged. "Who do you think got her the job?"

This did not make any sense. But then, she was staring into a punch bowl as if it were a crystal ball. And that didn't make any sense either.

"Look! There's your friend Rob again!"

Now he was on the other side of the pool table, sitting at the end of a black leather couch. Crowded up next to him was Penelope Jane.

Julie felt her stomach harden and her breaths come faster. "What's Rob doing with Penelope Jane?"

"Penny," Spade said.

And then Matthew came into view.

"Get away from him," Matthew told Penelope Jane.

"Why should I?"

"Because he's here with someone else."

"No, he's not!"

The red liquid swirled and, once again, Rory was there. He was still leaning against the pool table, but now Linda stood beside him.

Linda, in her slinky red dress.

Linda…who worked at the hardware store.

Linda knew that Rory had broken Julie's heart. So, naturally, they didn't talk about him. Except for when Julie asked if Rory would be at the annual Christmas party.

And this year, Linda had said he wouldn't be.

Linda had been wrong, but there you go. Even the best gossips can sometimes get it wrong.

Julie felt that tingling again, at the base of her neck.

She'd always assumed Rory would go away to school, eventually. In high school, that had been his plan.

He'd had a lot of plans. And—strange to remember this now—they'd always talked about *his* plans. About what *he'd* do after high school.

But never about what *she'd* do.

He'd talked about joining the army. Or going to business school. Or becoming a teacher.

She thought about that. About the possibility of Rory becoming a teacher. From this distance, from six years after high school, she didn't think he would make a good teacher.

"Listen," Punch said. "You can hear them talking."

. . . . .

"I told her you wouldn't be here," Linda said.

Rory stood up straight and his mouth fell open. "Why would you do that?"

"You know why." Linda crossed her arms over her chest. "Otherwise she wouldn't have come."

"I didn't want her to come!"

"She's back in town every Christmas." Linda scowled at him. "You can't tiptoe around her forever."

"Sure I can." He tugged at his suit jacket.

"It's time she knew about us," Linda said, deepening her tone.

Rory gripped the edges of the pool table and his eyes blinked rapidly. "Us?"

"Yes, us." Linda held her chin high. "We've been going out for six years. There is an *us*."

"I…uh…" Rory cupped the back of his neck with one hand. "I've been meaning to talk to you about that."

. . . . .

With her thoughts scrambling, Julie looked away from the scene in the rumpus room. All at once, a lightness fell over her and she felt almost giddy.

This was who she'd been worried about all this time?

This?

Punch stirred the punch, and it went back to being a concoction of lime and orange slices.

"We need a game of shinny," he said.

"You want to play shinny now?" Charlie covered his chubby face with his mittened hands, slowly shaking his head. "They were just getting to the good part!"

"We can head over to the community rink," Punch said.

"What's shinny?" Aretha asked, buffing her long red nails on her green shawl.

"Hockey," Punch said. "But without any rules."

"Or goalies," Charlie added.

"But we do have nets," Punch said. "And you need to be able to skate. Everyone here can skate."

"I can't." Spade folded her arms.

"You can watch," Punch told her.

"But don't you need to know something? Besides being able to skate?"

"Nope." Punch rocked back on his heels. "All you need to know is how to hold a stick. And maybe how to tap the puck once in a while."

"Julie?" Charlie touched her arm. "Do you want to come with us? Can you skate?"

"No. I mean, yes," she said. "Yes, I can skate. No, I don't want to go to the rink." Maybe later. "Not yet."

She felt as if she were waking up from a dream. And all she wanted to do was laugh. And to jump up and down.

All this time. All this wasted time.

She had to find Rob. "I'm going down to the rumpus room."

"To see Rory?" Punch asked.

"No," she answered, because Rory had quite suddenly become irrelevant.

"Now would be a good time," Punch told her. "It sounds like he's breaking up with Linda."

Aretha elbowed him. "Do you actually think she'd get back together with that creep?"

"Of course not." Punch frowned at Aretha. "And no elbowing."

"I have to find Rob."

"I think she's worried about Penelope Jane," Charlie said.

"Oh my stars! Call her Penny!"

"I'm *not* worried about Penelope—Penny—oh never mind."

Julie charged across the great room, reached the top of the stairs, grabbed hold of the handrail.

And tumbled all the way down.

· · · · ·

She woke up with a jerk.

"I've got you."

"Rob?"

"Who else would be hiding in this closet with you?"

They heard voices beyond the closet door.

"Did they come in here?"

"Yes," Linda said.

"That's Rory and Linda," Rob whispered in Julie's ear.

"I know."

She felt Rob's reassuring arms tighten around her.

"Rob?"

"What?"

"Kiss me?"

She felt him tense, and then relax again.

"Sure," he said. And he kissed her. A light kiss, his lips barely brushing hers. After a moment, he must have realized she was serious about kissing him, and the kiss deepened.

And deepened some more.

Then the closet door opened.

"They're in here," Matthew yelled over his shoulder.

"What are they doing in the closet?" Linda asked, coming into view.

"They're making out."

"Right," Linda said. She turned to look at someone near the door of the study. "Get over yourself, Rory. She obviously doesn't care about you."

Matthew looked down into the closet again. "We're going to the community rink to play a little shinny. Are you guys coming?"

"Skates?" Rob asked.

"The Bonninghams have lots of extra pairs of skates. Something will fit you. And it's stopped snowing."

"I see," Rob said, though he made no move to get up, or to let go of Julie.

"Oh, and besides that," Matthew continued, "there's a famous hockey coach here. Punch Somebody. He said he'd give us a few pointers."

"Matthew?" Rob asked, as he looked up from the floor.

"Yeah?"

"Close the door."

Matthew paused a second or two, and then the closet was dark again.

Rob and Julie heard the voices drift away.

"Did you want to go skating?" Julie asked.

"Not yet," Rob said. He adjusted his arms around her, making her more comfortable. Then, "Do you want me to kiss you again?"

Julie smiled, and that was when she knew everything would be all right. That was when she knew she had come home.

"Yes," she said. "I do."

After that, they stayed in the closet for a long, long time.

Dear Reader,

If you enjoyed
HOMECOMING MAGIC AT CHRISTMAS
you can help others find this story
by leaving a short review on Amazon.

Thanks!
Suzanne Stengl

Find more books by Suzanne Stengl here:

Sign up for Suzanne's Newsletter at
www.suzannestengl.com

About the Author

When I was a child, I shared a bedroom with three of my younger sisters. I used to tell them stories to help them fall asleep. Apparently the stories weren't particularly interesting, because they fell asleep before the stories ended. Unaware that they were sleeping, I would keep telling the story, until my mother called up the stairs. "Sue? They've gone to sleep." And then I would quietly finish the story in my head.

I didn't start writing down my stories until much later. In my last year of university, I collected all the reports from my Marketing Group and wrote up our study like a novel. My classmates liked it, and better, so did the prof.

Finally, after getting a degree in Commerce, I found a little two-line invitation to a romance writers organization in the back of the Writers Guild magazine. And I showed up. I had found my people.

"Suzanne Stengl has a lovely voice with a subtle hint of humor."
—*A.M. Westerling, author of A Knight for Love*

"Suzanne Stengl's descriptions and characters are really memorable."
—*Amy Jo Fleming, author of Death at Bandit Creek*

Printed in Great Britain
by Amazon

32186296R00029